Brenda L. Demmans was born in 1951 in Fergus, Ontario, Canada. She now lives in Mount Forest, Ontario, not too far from Fergus. She worked in various office jobs during her career, the longest being as a clerk at the local hospital, first in admissions and later in the emergency department. She raised one daughter and has a granddaughter who lives in the nearby town of Arthur, Ontario. She took a few writing courses at a local college when she was 40 years old, and this is her first piece of published writing.

TO MAKE YOU SMILE

BRENDA L. DEMMANS

AUSTIN MACAULEY PUBLISHERS™
LONDON • CAMBRIDGE • NEW YORK • SHARJAH

Ordering Information
Quantity sales: Special discounts are available on quantity purchases by corporations, associations, and others. For details, contact the publisher at the address below.

Publisher's Cataloging-in-Publication data
Demmans, Brenda L.
To Make You Smile

ISBN 9798889109082 (Paperback)
ISBN 9798889109099 (ePub e-book)

Library of Congress Control Number: 2024908843

www.austinmacauley.com/us

First Published 2024
Austin Macauley Publishers LLC
40 Wall Street, 33rd Floor, Suite 3302
New York, NY 10005
USA

mail-usa@austinmacauley.com
+1 (646) 5125767

For my loving husband, Karl who has been my supportive mate
for 32 years and counting!

Arnie Mines for Diamonds

Arnie the armadillo was just a pup at his grandfather's knee, listening to stories, when one evening, his grandfather told him a story about discovering diamonds. Since armadillos burrow for food in the soft forest floor of the Brazilian landscape, Arnie believed his grandfather had found a diamond when searching for insects sometime in his youth. He was not sure just what a diamond was, but understood that it was something precious, maybe even valuable. His grandfather had described them as bright and shiny —beautiful to behold.

Many years past and Arnie grew into a large 120-pound adult male armadillo, able to dig large burrows in the ground, at great speed while looking for insects and grubs to fill his hungry belly. While munching on a fat white grub one day, he recalled his grandfather's story about discovering diamonds. Arnie was not sure if his memory was correct, but he believed that he might find at diamond if he burrowed deep enough. Since he had nothing better to do this warm, sunny afternoon, he decided to try and mine for diamonds himself.

He donned a miner's helmet with a light positioned on the helmet strategically so he could see underground, as well as goggles to aid him in this endeavor. Then he had to decide where he should begin mining for diamonds.

Arnie looked East and West, North and South, up and down, and when he looked down, he said to himself, "Ah ha, this is where I should mine, in the ground, right here where I am standing."

Not very far into his dig, he was distracted by a fat June Bug by the name of Juliet. He asked Juliet if she had ever seen a diamond while laying her eggs in the soft Brazilian soil. The lovely creature asked Arnie what a diamond was. Arnie explained that it was something shinney but he himself had never seen one. The June Bug was sorry that she could not help him and was about to go on her way when Arnie instinctively shot out his sticky tongue and ate her! Opps! That was not very nice but she sure tasted good.

Arnie was working up a sweat, digging deeper and deeper into the earth when he came across Winston, an earth worm who was also working hard, processing his food by eating dirt. The dirt contained nutrients, that a worm's digestive system needed; this also helped Mother Nature aerate the soil so that plant roots could reach down deep and find water. Arnie wanted to ask Winston if he had ever seen a diamond, but as the worm was absorbed in his work, he did not want to disturb him, so he ate him!

Moving on even deeper, he stopped to wipe the dust from his goggles. Looking around his most recent tunnel, he was surprised to see a large white grub and was about to eat him when he thought he would first ask the grub if he had ever seen a diamond. The grub was not certain but told Arnie that perhaps he had seen a diamond some time ago, out near the roots of an old tree just ten meters to the west of their present location. Arnie was delighted, then he ate him!

Now Arnie had a full belly, he needed to rest, rolling up in a tight ball, he slept for a time before continuing to the old tree indicated by the tasty grub, Amie explored the area thoroughly but was disappointed once again.

That's enough of that, thought Arnie. With his sharp claws, he quickly burrowed his way out of the tunnel. Breathing in the fresh air and dusting off his armor coat he looked about him in wonder! What was this? There was a soft coating of white, cold fluff all over the ground. It sparkled in the sun! It hurt his eyes to look at it! It was so bright and shiny! DIAMONDS! Grandfather was right, there is such a thing as DIAMONDS!

Perkins the Praying Mantis

Perkins the Praying Mantis was a preacher, who lived in a blackberry bush, in a lovely garden in the small village of Greening. He held church service on a leafy branch of his blackberry bush for his insect friends' every Sunday morning.

Perkins was trying to catch the attention of Myrtle Mantis this beautiful Sunday in the month of May. He had a giant-sized crush on her, but she would not give him the time of day. Perkins had donned his black vest and clerical collar thinking he looked fine, and smiled broadly at Myrtle Mantis as she took her place on a leafy pew near the front of the branch.

Myrtle, however, was attracted to Conrad the Cricket and went out of her way to give Conrad one of her cutest smiles as he took his place. Seeing this, Perkins became green with envy. Conrad showed no interest in Myrtle, much to her chagrin. Perkins knew he would have to do something special if he were going to win Myrtle's hand, so he had a brilliant idea to serenade her with his voice in song.

Perkins the Praying Mantis started his sermon with a prayer, and another and another. Then the choir sang the hymn, "Holly, Holly, Holly." Jethro the June Bug sang in a loud buzz while Mary the mosquito hummed in the background. Perkins was about to sing so Myrtle Mantis would notice him. Before he could utter a note, he heard a strange sound from the second pew on his right. It rose into the rafters; it rang loud and clear, catching everyone's attention, especially Myrtle Mantis's. It was coming from Conrad Cricket. Conrad was winning the heart of Myrtle, and Perkins could do nothing to stop him. Conrad was rubbing his large back legs together, which brought forth the most pleasing noise. Everyone flapped their wings and jumped up and down. Myrtle swooned, startling Perkins. He rushed to her side with a glass of water and threw it in her face. Myrtle Mantis came too with a start and angrily shewed Perkins away. Thus, ending his hopes of ever attracting Myrtle Mantis. The choir sang on, the hole congregation joined in, causing the branches of the blackberry bush to shake until its' Berries fell to the ground.

Perkins said the final prayer, and all the insects flew, jumped, and crawled away to their homes.

Freeta the Feminist Pond Frog

When Freeta was just a small polliwog in the woodland swamp pond of Gorrie Bay, before she had legs, Foygle, a big boy polliwog, would bully her by pulling her tail and chasing her into the weeds, where she hid until he grew tired of bugging her.

Freeta and Foygle grew up; Freeta into a lovely pond frog, while Foygle turned into a large male bull frog who tried to rule the roost in Gorrie Bay swamp pond. Freeta challenged him at every turn, not seeing why a lady frog could not rule the pond creatures. Freeta was a feminist!

The creatures of Gorrie Bay swamp pond annually held the Gorrie Bay Olympics, in which Freeta and Foygle were strong competitors. Freeta participated in the Leapfrog event, jumping from Lilley pad to Lilley pad around the course. On this hot summer day after her Leapfrog event, Freeta grew thirsty and tried to open the water bottle she had strapped to her waist. After several frustrating attempts, she thinks, she is going to have to ask someone to open her water bottle for her. Looking around, she spotted Foygle lifting driftwood in the weightlifting competition. Should she ask him to open her water bottle? That bull frog is so full of himself, he'll probably gloat, she thought. He'll point out the fact that he is stronger than her. Freeta decided she would rather go thirsty.

Freeta was a feminist and competed with Foygle over every little and big thing. Freeta caught a fat fly for her lunch. Foygle, shooting out his long tongue, caught a larger one. Foygle claimed the choicest, most splendid Lilly pad for himself to sit on while Freeta perched on a smaller neighboring one.

Believe it or not they professed to love one another, and in the fall of that year, the Gorrie Bay swamp pond creatures held a large wedding for Freeta and Foygle.

The two called it a draw and shared a Lilly pad together on their honeymoon. In the spring, they became proud parents to several baby pollywogs and lived happily ever after in Gorrie Bay swamp pond.

Deadra the Dandelion

Deadra the dandelion was minding her own business one day, just doing what dandelions do: sunbathing on Mr. Brumble's front lawn when she was accosted by a bumble bee looking to steel her pollen. Deadra protested greatly by shaking her yellow head vigorously until the bee flew away in serch of another flower to plunder.

Relaxing after her wrestling match with the bee, she was blindsided by a lawn mower that passed by her with a loud humming from its motor. Deadra ducked her head on the second pass as the mower cut the neighboring grass, narrowly escaping with her life.

Mr. Brumble did not appreciate her subtle beauty and tried to kill her dead with a weed poison spray.

It is too bad that adults like Mr. Brumble do not appreciate dandelions as much as small children. Recently, Deadra saw Charlie, the neighbor's son picking a dandelion bouquet for his mother. Mrs. Wayne loved them. She even displayed them in an empty coffee jar on her dining room table for all to see.

Time passed, and Deadra's yellow petals turned gray. Some of her stamens blew away in a summer breeze. Deadra was worried that she would go bald if the wind was too strong. However, she met her demise at the hand of Charlie, who plucked her flower and blew her stamens up to the sky.

Deadra was not truly dead; however, her lovely green leaves were spared, her root lived to form another flower a few days later.

Deadra started a new family of dandelions in the neighbor's lawn with her stamen seeds.

One of the stamen seeds landed on the lawn of a widowed lady who did not use weed killer. Her yard was covered in wildflowers: violets, small daisies, and sweet white clove blossoms were scattered over her yard, both front and back as well as Deadra's baby dandelions.

Fustas the Fly

It was a lazy fall afternoon and Fustas the fly was hatching from his egg in a rotten potato at the bottom of Mrs. Gray's garbage can, outside her back door.

Fustas spread his gossamer wings and stretched his scrawny legs, then flew from the garbage can into Mrs. Gray's house through her open window, landing on a cherry pie just out of the oven, placed on the windowsill to cool

Mrs. Gray, seeing Fustas land on her cherry pie, got very upset and shewed him away. Fustas then landed on her kitchen counter, so Mrs. Gray got out her fly swatter and tried to swat Fustas. She tried several times, but each time Fustas escaped. Finally, Mrs. Gray took a time out to wash her dirty dishes that Fustas had crawled all over. She washed them good and placed them in the drain tray, where Fustas again walked on the clean plates.

Mrs. Gray decided to have a cup of tea. She sat at her kitchen table, covered with a pretty plastic tablecloth to keep it clean. Fustas walked across the clean tablecloth, flew up to Mrs. Grays teacup, and sat on its rim. Mrs. Gray took a sip of tea as Fustas flew away.

Fustas the fly went hunting for something to eat. Eventually he found himself in Mrs. Gray's bathroom. He took a tour around her toilet seat, then back in the kitchen again, he spotted the cherry pie. Fustas thought it would taste good so he landed on the pie and spit on a piece to make it suitable for his tummy.

Now that he was no longer hungry, Fustas slept in the sun on the windowsill until supper time.

Mrs. Gray had a big piece of cherry pie for her supper then went to bed. She turned the lamp on and got into her pajamas. Fustas followed Mrs. Gray to her bedroom, and seeing the light from the lamp, he commenced banging his head against the inside of the lampshade, knocking himself silly.

Mrs. Gray got into bed and turned out the light. Fustas settled on the ceiling and went fast asleep.

Gecko Love

Monti the gecko lived in a terrarium in Allen's house with his good friend Sheffield who was a gecko too. These two were inseparable and got along beautifully, each looking out for the other with acts of kindness, such as letting the other feed first on that offal orange mango powdery stuff Allen mixed with water to make a paste and set before them in a tiny gecko-sized dish.

Monti was a mottled cream color, and Sheffield – a taupe brown each with long tails, pointy noses and bulging eyes on the top of their heads. They are nocturnal creatures.

Monti and Sheffield loved to ware fascinator hats and dance in the evening in front of the Television with Allen. In the daytime Monti and Sheffield slept, sometimes upside down close together while clinging with the little suction cups on their feet to the glass of the terrarium. Often their naps were interrupted by Allen and his friend Corie who took them out for horseback riding on small plastic horses which bounced up and down, they were cowboys.

On Halloween, Allen placed the tiny geckos in a haunted house display on his mother's coffee table. Monti and Sheffield were not afraid.

At Christmas Monti and Sheffield had a bit of fun crawling through presents on a tin Santa Clause train display on that same coffee table.

The little geckos were very happy together for the most part, frolicking about their terrarium, playing with Allen and his friends but one day Allen went too far and took the pair for a swim in his wading pool in the backyard. The pair shed their tails as geckos do if they get really scared however it does not hurt them.

Monti and Sheffield lived a quiet life after that as Allen's mother had seen to it; they had no more great adventures when she was watching.

Everything You Ever Wanted to Know about Snails

It is a scientific fact that Mother Snails have lots of little baby snails, perhaps 50; many of these don't survive. They get sustenance from their mother snail by licking up the trail of silver milk she leaves behind her when she moves about doing her housework. This also ensures that the baby snails never get lost. The baby snails follow their mom back to a leafy tree at night where their mommy covers them with a leaf blankie because little snails do not have shells until they become teenagers.

Teenage snails develop beautiful, stripped shells in puberty, the male snail has the most colorful shell to attract the female snail. They eat leaves to get the calcium they need which aid in the production of the hard structure they carry on their short narrow slimy back; that is, their shell. Teenage snails attend trade school to learn how to earn a living when they become adults.

Snails congregate on the side of vinal clad houses, preferably white, in mating season, these homes are found mostly in North America; brick structures are also a good place for snails to mate, if they can't find a vinal clade house. After mating the father snail goes back to work while mother snail tends to her new brood of baby snails and works part time as baby snail sitter for single snail

Mothers that have lost their husbands in the fish tanks of the world, Due to lack of oxegan, (fish owners often put too many water creatures in their fish tanks.) Also, the female snails work as tradeschool teachers for teenage snails.

Father snails may work as aquarium cleaners but are in great demand by the Postal Service to deliver the Snail Mail. The Post Office pays the snails for their work by raising the price of stamps every year.

Snails are industrious creatures but in recent years with the advent of social media they are being put out of work at the Post Office. Please continue to write letters the old-fashioned way occasionally, in support of the Snails of the world so they do not become extinct. Also advocate for danger pay for those Snails working as aquarium cleaners.

NOTE
PAY
TAX

The Forest Creatures Are Taxed

Siggy the red tailed squirl was a thrifty fellow, always squireling nuts away for those cold days of winter. Siggy hid nuts under leaves and up trees; Siggy got his knees dirty burring nuts in the ground.

Siggy was proud of himself, he never went hungry because his memory was so sharp that he always or almost always remembered where he hid his nuts although he wondered sometimes at all the acorn trees, he saw sprouting up in the forest each spring.

Life was good! Until one day when he saw a posting on the big spruce tree in the glen where he liked to hang out with the other woodland critters; Billy the baby deer and his mother, Sidnie the snake who liked to sunbathe in the glen and the other forest dwellers. Everyone was crowded around the poster reading what it had to say.

To everyone's consternation, it was a decree that all the forest creatures were now required to pay taxes to Mr. Brown Bear who was the largest forest dweller of them all and liked to throw his weight around.

Well now, what were they going to do about this thought Siggy the squirl? He was not going to part with any of his nuts that he had worked so hard to acquire. Siggy was not going to give in to that lazy Brown Bears demands.

Mrs. Deer was astonished! How could she gather up enough grass for herself and her fawn let alone feed Mr. Brown Bear too? This is impossible, she thought.

Sidnie the snake hissed, "Never,"
All the woodland creatures protested greatly!
Siggy had an idea!

He got all the forest creatures together and had them make signs from tree bark to picket the bears dwelling place. Back and forth they marched in front of Brown Bear's Cave, chanting...

"Lazy Bear, Lazy Bear, we won't pay your Tax!"
We are not afraid of you and will not do what you ask.
We will not share, Mr. Brown Bear!

Brown Bear was too tired and lazy to argue with all the creatures of the forest, so he rolled over and went back to sleep. When the forest dwellers found they had got the best of Mr. Brown Bear, Siggy went back to hunting nuts. Mother deer and Billy the fawn munched on grass. Sidnie the snake went back to his Sunbathing, everyone else went back to whatever they had been doing and the forest was peaceful again.

The Crow that Goes to Mexico

As the crow flies, Carly the crow was "directionally challenged." Carly lived in Ontario, Canada, most of the year. In the fall she migrated South to Carolina in the USA, where she vacationed over the cold months of the year. However, as Carly was directionally challenged, she often found herself in some other county or state. She was in another state all right, when, this year while on her migration vacation she ended up in Mexico. Last year she spent her winter months in Cuba, an island in the Caribbean, it was a nice place to visit but that was not her intended destination. Where was Carolina anyway, or even the USA for that matter. Boy! These long trips were tiring! She must have made a left turn when she was supposed to make a right at that corn field back there in Ohio, a state just south of Ontario Canada, or maybe it was when she crossed the border into the USA that Carly got her wires crossed. She had to make the best of it though now that she found herself here in Mexico. She was seeing a lot of the world and so far, Carly hadn't crossed any oceans; she believed that was a positive thing.

Carly decided to look around this new place called Mexico. It was a bit more tropical than she desired and the vegetation was not familiar, all was not lost! Carly saw a corn field and took full advantage by feasting on a tasty corn cob. This was much better than the roadkill that was her most recent meal. Carly was a bit fastidious and only lowered herself to eat roadkill when there was absolutely nothing else to eat.

Carly spent some time resting on a telephone pole, (Carly heard the locals call it a siesta,) before turning around and getting her bearings, so she thought; she flew North. Carly was headed back to Ontario in hopes to get there some time next spring.

After flying for two days Carly found herself in California, a state on the west coast of the USA. She landed near a beach on the Pacific Coast and was quite taken with the sport of surfing. Carly tried hitching a ride with a young boy catching a wave. He brushed Carly off. Obviously, she was not close to the Ontario boarder and Canada yet. Carly flew on!

Next stop was British Columbia, Canada. totally on the other side of the country than she wanted to be, did they have crows living here?

Carly was weary; it was now June, and she should have been back in her home province weeks ago. Looking around her she liked what she saw, green trees, lakes and telephone poles, perhaps this year she could settle down her on the West Coast of Canada, then next year she could try and find Carolina to spend her winter migration vacation like other Ontario Crows and just maybe in the spring she would find her way back to Ontario.

Blind Malcolm Segel

"What?" "Where am I?" "Is that rock and roll music that is playing so loud it is hurting my ears?"

Malcolm Segel found himself on stage in the middle of a late-night rock concert in Victoria Park, put on by the Optimus Club of Fergus, a small town in Ontario, Canada. At first, he was stunned and didn't know what was happening. Malcolm Segel was blind; he wore thick-lens spectacles and walked with a white cane. He ran in circles, nearly getting stepped on, until he made his escape.

Malcolm was always getting lost, just the other day, while burrowing under the ground, he hit his head on the pavement of Union Street when trying to come up for air. Then, while making his way out of that mess, he nearly fell into a deep manhole in the same street. Malcolm panicked, he squealed, a friendly mouse heard him and came to his rescue. The mouse, Chalmers, was his name, discussed with Malcolm his situation and the two came up with a plan.

Malcolm needed a service dog. This dog would lead Malcolm around so he wouldn't get lost again. So Malcolm Segel and Chalmers the mouse approached a passing Spaniel being walked on a leash. Chalmers was the spokes mouse for the pair, as moles are introverts and seldom speak. The Spaniel was surprised that Chalmers would ask him to be a seeing-eye dog for a mole and passed on by while saying that he needed someone to lead him and could not help Malcolm.

Next, Chalmers spotted a Great Dane but rejected that idea right away. That dog was way too big he would step on Malcolm Segel or eat him, which would be terrible.

Malcolm Segel and Chalmers the mouse put their heads together; they needed to find a service dog for Malcolm the mole, who was a small furry rodent about the same size as a mouse. They decided a miniature Chihuahua was the dog they needed. However, neither one knew where to find a Chihuahua.

Malcolm Segel was disappointed. "What was he going to do?" He had nearly gotten himself killed so many times. Once he even came up in a large puddle; gasping and flailing about, he managed to extract himself from that situation. He did not want to repeat his near-drowning. Also, on many occasions, he had come close to being run over by motor vehicles.

Malcolm Segel expressed his grief and worry to Chalmers the mouse, Chalmers felt sorry for Malcolm and, after much thought, decided to be Malcolm Segels' seeing-eye mouse.

Bob the Dung Beetle Bug Is Bald!

Bob the Dung Beetle Bug was bald. This distressed him greatly; his self-esteem was as low as it could possibly be. In his dreams, he was gorgeous with long, flowing black wavy hair which attracted all the Lady Dung Beetle Bugs. Bob believed his baldness was holding him back in his career. He was a lowly employee on the ladder of life, rolling dung and storing it for food. Bob the Dung Beetle desired to be promoted to supervisor so that he would not have to get his claws dirty rolling dung balls and burying them for future use.

Bob tried several remedies for his bald condition, but nothing had worked. He made wigs out of flower petals and acorn caps, but the Lady Dung Beetles laughed at him. Another time, he went to a Witch Doctor and got a treatment for baldness that tasted like mud. He spat it out and forgot about finding a cure for his baldness.

Bob the Dung Beetle Bug was despondent. He wore sunglasses and hid in dark allies to avoid the ridicule he supposed would come from the Lady Dung Beetles if he were to approach one of them and ask for a date.

Quietly, he went about his work rolling dung balls to make a living. Going unnoticed by his superiors, he did not entertain hopes for promotion.

Bob was mistaken, however! There was a little Lady Dung Beetle who worked close beside him that he had overlooked. Beverly the Dung Beetle was rolling her ball of dung one day and bumped into Bob with her ball of dung. Startled, the two took a step back and looking at each other. It was love at first sight.

Bob and Beverly became an item after that. Bob no longer worried about being bald; his confidence grew, and he eventually got a promotion to supervisor of the Dung Rolling Dung Beetles.

Dung Beetles do not have hair on their heads; none of them do!

The Tandori Story

Tandori are fat little critters, round and rollie polly with long tails, bulging eyes and blue in color. They live exclusively in Elmira Ontario, Canada and are quite rare indeed. Their main source of sustenance is maple syrup from maple trees which are plentiful in and around Elmira. They hatch in the spring from small, microscopic size green eggs that the female Tandori lays in the hollows between maple tree bows and branches.

Each spring, the baby Tandories like to play amongst the maple keys on the ground in the maple tree forest.

The people of Elmira put out buckets to catch the tree syrup; the Tandories take full advantage of this practice by swimming around in the buckets of syrup and drinking their fill at the same time, to the frustration of the maple syrup farmers.

The Tandori are threatening the livelihood of the local farmers. The farmers hunt them with great enthusiasm as they have found the plump little Tandori are tasty when grilled on their maple syrup fires that they build to reduce the tree syrup to make table syrup that they put on their toast for their breakfast.

The Tandori are hard to catch, however, they move fast; therefore, they are considered a delicacy to the folks in Elmira.

In April each year, during the maple syrup harvest, the Elmira farmers sponsor a Maple Sugar Festival. Thousands of spectators come from miles around to sample the locally produced maple syrup on pancakes. They also serve up grilled Tandori which is a popular treat for the tourists also.

By the way, the Tandori are invisible.

Shy Brenda

In 1951, a baby girl weighing 8 pounds and 5 ounces was born to Charles and Pauline Morrison, who were teenagers at the time. The birth took place in the original Groves Hospital building in Fergus, Ontario, Canada. Groves Hospital gained renown as it was named after its founder, Doctor Groves, who performed the first appendectomy that saved Charles' life and many others. Seven years later, it played a crucial role in saving his baby girl's life as well. At the age of seven, she required a highly unusual appendectomy.

Their doctor, Doctor Wilson, informed Brenda's parents, as they had named her, that she would not survive without the surgery due to severe abdominal pain. Despite lacking enough money to cover the procedure, they agreed out of desperation. At the time, there was no concept of healthcare as we know it today.

Charles and Pauline brought the baby to Charles' parents' house, where they resided until they could find a place of their own. To their dismay, they discovered their beautiful baby girl was cross-eyed – a condition caused by weak muscles in the eyes causing them to turn inward. They took their child to the doctor who told them Brenda would grow out of this condition so there was nothing to worry about and, fortunately, at the age of one her eye condition cured.

Also, Pauline was unable to breastfeed the baby, so she fed her a formula mixed with water. However, this formula caused Brenda to gain too much weight. It was later discovered that all the babies fed this formula were overweight. Pauline promptly stopped using the formula, and Brenda lost the excess weight.

The young couple, Charles and Pauline, found themselves facing both financial and spiritual challenges early in their marriage. Seeking guidance, they turned to a nearby baptist church a few years after their baby, Brenda, was born. Brenda, wearing a red coat with leggings and a matching hat, clutched her cherished possession—a white rabbit fur muff—as they approached the church for the first time.

Despite her parents' encouragement, Brenda was terribly shy and reluctant to leave the car. However, a compassionate church member approached and persuaded her to come inside by mentioning other children in Sunday school who would admire her muff. Reluctantly, Brenda entered the church, where the small family was warmly welcomed into the congregation.

Brenda soon found solace in attending Sunday school and participating in the choir, finding joy in the spiritual community. However, when she turned 13, her Sunday school teacher asked her to read from the Bible aloud. Brenda, who struggled with reading and was embarrassed by her difficulty, adamantly refused. This refusal marked the end of Brenda's attendance at church, and many years would pass before she felt ready to seek spiritual guidance again.

Despite her initial withdrawal from organized religion, Brenda's journey with spirituality would continue to evolve over time, eventually leading her back to seek solace and guidance for herself.

The young couple, Charles and Pauline, settled into a few rooms in the town of Fergus, on Saint George Street, under the care of their landlady, Mrs. Lamb. Mrs. Lamb, described as a kind-hearted woman, had a reputation for helping people in need, particularly during the difficult years of the 1930s' Great Depression.

One day, as Pauline and her 4-year-old daughter Brenda sat on the back porch of Mrs. Lamb's home, a beggar approached the door seeking food. It was a common sight during those tough times for men to travel from town to town in search of work, often hopping onto freight trains like the Canadian Pacific Railway without money for fare, and relying on the kindness of strangers for sustenance along the way. Pauline engaged the beggar in conversation while Mrs. Lamb prepared him a sandwich. Through their interaction, Pauline learned that the man had left his wife and five children behind in Scarborough in his quest for employment.

Brenda's parents lived at Mrs. Lamb's until they bought their first home shortly after Charles acquired work at Beatty Brothers factory in Fergus, Ontario, in the forge and press department, where they made steel parts for the farm equipment the factory produced, as well as parts for the first wringer washing machines ever made. Their home was a small 3-bedroom frame house on Colquhoun Street that was purchased through the generosity of a benevolent neighbor Mrs. Lamb knew, in the town of Fergus, just a 10-minute walk from Beatty Brothers factory where Charles worked. Pauline stayed home and kept house while taking care of 4-year-old Brenda and her new baby brother, Rodney.

The small house was not yet heated by a furnace. The couple planned to install one later when they had saved enough money, as buying on credit was not popular back then. Currently, the house was still heated by two wood stoves. In the kitchen, there was a large cast iron range used for cooking and heating water, which Pauline diligently kept shining with blacking — a liquid she used to clean and preserve it. In the living room, there was a small but effective pot belly stove with four legs. Each morning,

Charles would rise first and stoke the stoves with a log or two to rekindle the embers left from the previous night's fire. Following, Pauline would wake up a bit later, prepare breakfast for the two of them, and pack Charles' lunch—a sandwich with cold cuts, perhaps an apple if in season, and usually a homemade cookie or pastry, as Pauline was renowned for her baking. After bidding him farewell with a kiss and hug, she would then tend to her children, getting them ready for the day ahead.

One particularly cold winter morning, Pauline brought Brenda and Rodney downstairs beside the potbelly stove in the living room to dress, thinking it would be warmer there. Brenda was delighted to find that her mommy was going to dress her in boys' clothes, a departure from her usual attire of frilly dresses with puff sleeves and bows, which was customary in the early 1950s. That morning, she would wear her brother's clothes—navy corduroy pants with plaid lining at the pant cuffs to match the red plaid flannel shirt. Pauline had wisely purchased these clothes for her daughter to keep her warm that winter. Brenda, being a bit of a tomboy, relished the idea of wearing pants.

After dressing, the two children hurried into the kitchen and climbed up on the vinyl-covered chairs at the formica table to be served cream of wheat cereal topped with brown sugar and milk, delivered daily by the milkman. Brenda wasn't particularly fond of cream of wheat, but she enjoyed brown sugar. She would eat the top off the cereal and leave the part not covered by brown sugar, then tell her Mom she was not hungry. Pauline would warn Brenda that she would be hungry later and point out the fact that Rodney ate all his cereal.

Until Brenda was 5 years old, she shared a bedroom in that small cozy little house with her brother Rodney who was 3 years younger than her. At that time, she got her own room, and in that room, there was a window seat which Brenda loved to sit in on Saturday mornings when her parents were sleeping late. On cold winter mornings, her single-pane window was covered with beautiful fern designs which she was told were created by Jack Frost. Jack Frost was well known in the 50s to poor people who had single-paned windows. These windows did not retain heat well, and the condensation that formed on them made beautiful frost patterns, hence the name Jack Frost. Brenda believed there really was a little ice man with a sharp, pointy nose and ears, wearing a tall hat, who, in a way, looked like a little mouse, all made of ice, and who came in the night to paint those beautiful designs on her window.

On a particularly cold winter morning, one Christmas eve, Brenda got up early and, looking out her window as usual, was startled to see sleigh tracks in the snow on their front lawn. She hurried into her parents' room and, looking out of their window, loudly proclaimed that Santa had come to their home during the night because he had left sleigh tracks in the snow on the lawn in front of their house. "Come see, Dad," said Brenda.

Charles and Pauline, still in bed, laughed to themselves and said, "Sweetheart, I don't think those are sleigh tracks left by Santa's sleigh. Perhaps they were left yesterday when you were sliding down the hill yourself at the front of our house." Brenda was disappointed, but her parents reassured her that Santa Claus would surely come that night.

That same Christmas eve, Charles had to go to work on a farm outside the community of Fergus to earn extra money to pay for the children's Christmas presents that year. He had worn out his rubber boots and commented just before leaving that he truly needed a new pair of boots. Brenda and Rodney started jumping around and gesturing to Pauline while pointing to a large present under the Christmas tree; the gift was for their father. Pauline looked at the excited faces of her children and decided to give her husband an early Christmas present – a pair of rubber boots. Charles opened the gift quickly, put on the boots, thanked his loved ones profusely, and headed off to work.

The children spent some considerable time that Christmas eve looking at the beautiful Christmas tree and the presents beneath it. The spruce tree was adorned with silver tinsel, red garlands, and Brenda's favorite lights that looked like candles with bubbles floating about inside. Pauline soon hurried the two young ones off to bed but just before they went upstairs, she had them put out a glass of milk with two of her homemade cookies for Santa.

The next morning, Brenda and Rodney were awake early around 6:00 AM. Their parents knew how excited they were to see what Santa had brought them, so they got up early and turned up the heat as they now had central heating supplied by an oil furnace. Once the house was warm, Pauline called the children to come downstairs and see what Santa had brought them.

Brenda and Rodney came charging down the stairs in their pajamas, ran into the living room, and then froze at the sight of their gifts displayed attractively; Rodney's on the sofa and Brenda's in Charles' large burgundy armchair. They were not wrapped but arranged nicely for the children to take in. Every Christmas they would get a new toothbrush and an orange in their stocking, which was pinned to the back of the sofa, one of Charles' large gray wool work socks for each of them. Also, there were walnuts and Christmas candies in their stockings. The candies were hard mints that stuck together in the package, in colors of bright green, red, and white stripes that Brenda did not like. She gave them to her father who thanked her and popped one in his mouth.

Brenda got a large baby doll with real baby clothes, it was life-size, an art kit with pencil crayons, a sketchpad, and watercolor paints. The art kit would always be Brenda's favorite Christmas gift. Rodney, upon investigating his gifts, discovered to his joy a red fire truck with a real bell and rubber tires which he would later take apart to supply his imaginary garage where he fixed his cars and trucks. Also, for both the children, their father had cut wooden blocks from scrap that he found at his place of work to make play blocks for the kids.

While the children were playing with their toys, Pauline and Charles proceeded to make Christmas dinner by stuffing a large turkey from their freezer. They prepared roast potatoes, carrots, and rutabaga. For dessert, Pauline made suet pudding, a recipe handed down from her mother, filled with candied cherries that also called for molasses and suet, which she steamed and covered with a brown sugar sauce. At lunchtime, the little family shared this feast every Christmas.

The Morrison family continued to prosper over the coming years.

Brenda loved going shopping with her mother and brother, Rodney. One day, they walked downtown Fergus to Stedman's store. Pauline left Brenda and Rodney outside the store, with Rodney sitting in his stroller looking like a doll with his black hair combed up to form a curl on top of his head. Brenda was drawn to the gum ball machine outside the store, hoping she would later get a nickel to put in the machine and get a red gum ball to chew. She started climbing on the wheel of the stroller and fell off, hitting her face on the windowsill of Stedman's store. She cut her eyelid, which later left a scar. When her mother came out of the store, she was upset to see the blood on Brenda's face and red spring coat, but Brenda was not crying. After Pauline took some Kleenex and pressed it to her wound, which was not serious, Brenda was just fine.

Inside Stedman's store, Pauline had bought a pattern for making little dresses and shirts for her children. Years later, Brenda would love to look at those patterns in Stedman's herself and would also learn to sew on her mother's sewing machine. Pauline was very crafty; she also knit sweaters for the children.

After shopping at Stedman's, they went across the street to Scott's bakery, where their mother purchased some crusty bread that Scott's bakery was famous for. Brenda saw many delicious treats and pastries there that she asked her mother to buy. However, Pauline, being a very good baker herself, told Brenda that she would make her some date squares when they got home for supper. They headed home, with Rodney in his stroller and Brenda holding on to the handle. Up Saint Andrews Street, across Tower Street, past the big, tall stone United Church on the corner of Tower and Saint Andrew, then up the long hill home.

Grocery shopping on Friday night after Charles received his paycheck was a special treat for the Morrison family. They shopped at Guthrie's grocery store in the center of town, a store that was very small compared to today's grocery stores. The store supplied baskets for their customers. Pauline would carry a basket and her grocery list, while Charles held onto Brenda's hand and carried Rodney. Some of their special treats included an eight-pack of small cereal boxes put out by the Kellogg's Company for the children, containing Frosted Flakes, Corn Flakes, Rice Krispies, and Cheerios. The children often fought over who would get the first pick, as they both wanted Frosted Flakes. For Charles, Pauline would buy a package of bologna and a can of sardines; Charles would share his sardines with Brenda as soon as they got home, even before the groceries were unpacked, as no one else in the family liked them.

Pauline, who loved to bake, would buy cherry or blueberry pie filling to make her pies, dates for her date squares, Crisco, eggs, and flour for her pie crust. She did not buy any other fruit or vegetables as she preserved vegetables from her garden in the fall; pickled beets, mustard beans, spaghetti sauce, pickles, and relish. Fruit would come on sale, such as peaches and pears, which they also preserved. One year, Charles and Pauline received a gift: two bushels of pears from their neighbor's pear tree, which they preserved in their kitchen. Brenda had the stomach flu at the time and was sick in bed upstairs; the smell of pears and cloves permeated the house and exacerbated Brenda's condition. It would be decades before she could ever stand the scent or taste of pears again.

Charles decided to wallpaper the bedrooms of their home with pink, blue, and cream floral paper. He asked Brenda to help him by holding the paper face down on a table so he could paint white glue on the back to adhere it to the wall. After a short time, Charles told Brenda she could go out to play until supper was ready. Putting her coat on again and her shoes, she ran out the front door, up the short hill to the sidewalk in front of their home where she stopped abruptly at the sight of a very large turtle, to her surprise.

Quickly, she ran back into the house hollering, "Dad, Dad, come quick, come see what I have found." Her father thought something terrible had happened; he hurried down the stairs, dropping his roll of wallpaper on the table, and out the door he flew after Brenda, her leading all the way. There he beheld a turtle, a large snapping turtle. He smiled and said, "Now what are we going to do with this fellow." Putting his hand to his chin, he pondered this. "Ha," Charles said. "I know what we'll do, we will put him in Mom's wash tub that she does her laundry in." Pauline had a new wringer washer from Beatty Brothers but also scrubbed very dirty clothes with a cake of Sunlight soap on a washboard in her wash tub than hung them out to dry on her clothesline."

Charles got the wash tub, put some water in it, and set it beside the house then he put the turtle in very carefully. Pauline and Rodney came out to have a look at this awesome sight before going in for supper. After a supper of boiled chicken followed by cherry pie, Brenda went out to check on the turtle. The turtle was gone. She told her father and he said, "I think that turtle climbed out of the tub and headed back down to the river where he lives." The Grand River was down the hill behind their home just a short few hundred yards on the other side of Mr. Noble's little cottage built onto the side of the hill, on Johnston Street.

Brenda and Rodney also helped their father Charles with his small collection of livestock. Even though they lived in the town of Fergus, the laws allowed people of the time to raise small animals like chickens and rabbits. Charles had a chicken run built on the back of the garage and under the garage, there was a room for their nests where the chickens could lay eggs. Also, he built a small shed at the back of their property where he raised large white rabbits to sell at the Stockyards, a sales barn where farmers brought livestock to auction off each week in Kitchener, Ontario; this provided a small profit for their savings.

In the fall, Charles would enlist the help of his family to slaughter the chickens and some of the rabbits to put in the freezer for food over the winter months. On one of these occasions, Brenda, Rodney, and some of their cousins were watching Charles and his brother Arnold cut the heads off the chickens using an axe and chopping block. One of the chickens, having its head cut off, jumped off the chopping block and started to run around, to the children's amazement, with no head. Charles explained to the children that the chicken's brain had sent a message to the chicken's body to run away quick just before he chopped off its head, and the message got through to its body just in time, so it still ran away even with no head. The chicken did eventually die after its short run, and then these beheaded chickens were passed on to the women in the family, Pauline and her sister Barbara, to dunk in hot water until they could pull the feathers off. The men would clean the innards out of the chickens and wash them; the women would package the chickens and rabbits for the freezer.

"All this may sound gruesome to some people of today who are not used to such goings-on; however, back in the '50s and earlier, this was a common practice in order to provide food for their families, and so did not shock the children all that much."

She attended kindergarten at James McQueen School in Fergus, and her mother, Pauline, took her to school on the first day. Brenda wouldn't sit at a desk like the other children, so Miss Tyee, the teacher, brought a little chair for her to sit beside her mother. Pauline had a difficult time trying to get Brenda to go to kindergarten by herself. It was a long walk from Colquhoun Street, up Breadalbane Street to Saint George where the public school stood.

Pauline's sister Barbara lived only a block away and had a daughter the same age as Brenda, so the two sisters arranged for Brenda and Connie to walk to school together for a time, until Brenda felt safe enough to walk the few blocks to school on her own.

Even though Brenda was one of the oldest children in her kindergarten class because her birthday was in January at the beginning of the year, she found it difficult. The teacher, Miss Tyee, was teaching the children how to tie their shoes using a large wooden shoe with laces in it. Each child had to take a turn until they could successfully tie a neat bow in those laces. Brenda took a considerable time to learn how to tie that shoe, which embarrassed her. Eventually, she did tie that dumb old wooden shoe that looked like the nursery rhyme about the old woman who lived in a shoe and had so many children she didn't know what to do.

"Nursery rhymes were very popular many years ago. They were short little rhyming stories, sometimes even offensive according to today's standards. For instance, the old woman who lived in the shoe had so many children she didn't know what to do. Eventually, she spanked them all soundly and sent them to bed. Today, in the 21st century, in Western civilization, spanking is frowned upon and could even get you brought before a court of law."

Another challenging moment arose when the teacher would have each child sing in front of the class. It seemed to Brenda, who was quite shy, that the teacher was always singling her out, although it was the same for all the children. Brenda initially refused to sing, but eventually, being the last one, she did sing. She sang a few lines from the song "Robin in the Rain." Brenda did not look at anyone while singing. "Brenda was so shy she never looked people in the eye but usually hung her head and looked at the floor when someone talked to her directly." The teacher was delighted and told Brenda that she had a lovely singing voice. "Brenda would later sing solos in music class taught by Mr. Noon, the music teacher, and get the highest marks in the class. She sang in choirs and loved it, but she always remained timid." In any event, kindergarten was a precursor to her school years, which she would find challenging because of her shyness.

After school, the children in the West End of Fergus, where Brenda and her family lived, gathered at the park, just minutes away from Brenda's home. She would play alone most of the time on the swings in the park. She would swing for long periods, moving higher and higher until she believed she could touch the leaves of the silver maple tree in the center of the park. There were teeter-totters, monkey bars, and a grassy area where the neighborhood children played scrub baseball in the summertime. In the winter, that large grassy area was made into an ice rink by the local fire department, who used their hoses to pump water onto the field, which froze to make an ice rink where the neighborhood children played hockey.

One winter, when Brenda was 5 years old and the snow was deep on the ground, Pauline dressed Brenda in a blue one-piece felt snowsuit that was so warm Brenda would sweat even on very cold days. The snowsuit was purchased from a second-hand store in town where Pauline shopped frequently. That snowsuit was paired with a cozy hat and warm wool mittens her aunt Barbara had knit for her for Christmas. Brenda loved those mittens because no matter how many snowmen she built, those yellow mittens would not get wet as quickly as her old mittens that she had lost. One cold winter day when Brenda, her brother Rodney, her cousins Connie and Leslie from Johnson St around the corner from Brenda's home were making snowmen at her house, she had to go to the washroom very badly. She hurried into the house and hollered to her mother to help her get that one-piece thick felt snowsuit off that made it almost impossible for her to move. "Nowadays one would compare it to the Michelin Man; that's how she felt." Brenda hated that snowsuit and she squirmed and fought to get the zipper undone but peed her pants before her mother could get there to help her out of it. It was a blessing in disguise. The snowsuit was ruined, and she never had to wear it again.

Brenda grew strong by climbing the monkey bars and swinging hand over hand while hanging from them. Her brother Rodney and his friends particularly liked the teeter-totter.

The teeter-totter was very old, so no one could be blamed for carelessly breaking it. However, it did get broken one day, and a local bully confronted Rodney in the park, accusing him of breaking the teeter-totter. He told Rodney that he would not be able to play in the park ever again. Brenda was present and stood up to the bully, telling him that he had no right to keep Rodney out of the park. "Who did he think he was anyway?" He kicked Brenda in the shin, but she did not cry. Despite usually avoiding confrontations, Brenda stuck up for her little brother. Brenda was so angry that she held her tears in until Rodney and her crossed the street and were halfway home. The bully was so startled that a girl did not cry and ran away when he kicked her that he left the park and did not go back. It seems that when someone stands up to a bully, they are often the ones to back down.

On weekends, the little Morrison family would get a special treat at the Fergus Dairy at the top of the hill on Breadalbane Street. Their treat was an ice cream cone for everyone in the family. They called it Ice Cream Sunday, as it was usually on Sunday that they went for ice cream in Charles' first car, a second-hand Ford with a broken door latch on the passenger side. Brenda once fell out of it one day while riding with her father when she was just 4 years old. She was saved by her father's quick thinking. He grabbed her by the ankle as she toppled out and hauled her back into the car, uttering a few choice words in his fear.

The dairy on Breadalbane Street served as the primary supplier of milk to the community of Fergus back in the 1950s. Each morning, a horse pulling a covered wagon would deliver bottles of milk to the doors of homes that requested it. Brenda's parents would leave change in the empty milk bottle from the previous day at the front door. The milkman would then replace the empty bottle with a full one. The liter-sized glass bottles of milk had cream on the top, which Charles liked to skim off for his coffee in the morning.

Most weekends, Brenda and Rodney would visit their grandparents, Clifford and Viola Morrison, at their home on Saint George Street near James McQueen School. Brenda adored their large old house, believed to be the first home ever built in Fergus. The house sat on a large lot surrounded by a meticulously tended garden, cared for by Clifford, who worked as a gardener for Beatty Brothers in Fergus in later years. Cabbages grew in straight rows beside peppers, tomatoes, and lettuce. Tall gladiolus thrived next to a wire fence edging the garden. At the back of the lot, Clifford had a chicken coop and rabbit hutch from which he supplied meat for his family. During the Great Depression of the 1930s, Clifford took on any job he could find to earn money. One of these jobs involved butchering cattle and curing meat for farmers who needed provisions for the winter. Viola gave birth to seven children, five boys and two girls. Viola herself was a twin at birth, but due to her parents' circumstances, she was given up for adoption to the Porterfield family of Orangeville. The Porterfield family lived on a farm off Highway 10 near Celadon, Ontario, not far from where Clifford was raised. Today, the Porterfield farm has been taken over by Teen Ranch, a refuge and spiritual training site for troubled young people. Clifford and Viola met at church box socials, where young single women prepared picnic lunches for young men to bid on. Clifford and Viola soon married and moved to Fergus, where they lived their entire lives.

Upon entering Grandma Viola's front door, a large blackboard made of slate adorned the right wall, positioned high up where Brenda could not reach it. Grandma Viola would often bring a chair for Brenda to stand on so she could draw pictures on the blackboard. Later in life, Brenda would receive several prizes and monetary awards for her artwork. On the left side of the entry hall was a door leading to what used to be a spacious dining room, which Grandpa Clifford had converted into a chick hatchery. Brenda frequently visited this room to watch the chicks hatch from their eggs, observing them with rapt attention as they scurried around under the warmth of heat lamps in a large box built by Clifford.

Passing through a small living room from the hall, where Grandpa Clifford often sat to smoke his pipe while watching TV, Brenda once observed his smoking routine with fascination. She watched him tap his pipe on the ashtray, fill the bowl with tobacco, light it with a match, and puff on it, blowing smoke out of his mouth. Finding the kitchen at the back of the house equally intriguing, Brenda discovered many wonders during her visits to Grandma and Grandpa's house. The kitchen featured a large built-in square table in the middle, accommodating all nine members of the family. An enamel sink with a water pump, reminiscent of farm life, stood in one corner, accompanied by a large cast iron wood stove with an oven at the back. Next to the stove was a cupboard for dishes. In another corner, Grandma Viola's rocking chair sat beside a window, where she would often chat with her canary in a nearby cage. Viola had trained the canary to say "Hello" as she worked around the kitchen. Additionally, a white enamel icebox occupied another corner, kept cool by regular deliveries of large blocks of ice stored in a wagon filled with sawdust. This was how Grandma Viola preserved her butter and milk.

During one of Brenda's many visits to her grandparents' house, she had the chance to explore the upstairs area. There wasn't much of note, just several small bedrooms, five in total. Upon inspection, she noticed that the upstairs was sparsely furnished and quite cold. However, one thing caught her curiosity: a door that, when opened, revealed a secret stairwell, with voices audible from below. This frightened her, prompting her to quickly close the door and return downstairs to her grandmother. Brenda never mentioned finding the door to anyone, but it lingered in her thoughts. In later years, she discovered that it led to the other side of the house where Clifford and Viola's oldest son, Herbert, and his family lived. While it was merely a passageway between family residences, Brenda found joy in imagining it as a portal to a mysterious and enchanted world during her youth.

Grandma Viola was known for her baking skills, and she was also a talented cook. On one visit, Brenda accompanied her grandmother down Tower Street to the Co-op to retrieve a large roast of beef to cook in their wood stove. The Co-op rented storage space in a community freezer for a small fee. Viola's specialties included cherry pie and large oatmeal cookies filled with dates, both of which Brenda adored.

Brenda cherished her visits to her grandparents' house, especially during times when her mother, Pauline, was expecting another baby. During one such occasion, Brenda stayed with them for a week while her brother Rodney stayed with their uncle Arnold, aunt Barbara, and cousins Connie and Leslie. This arrangement allowed their father, Charles, to focus on work and visit Pauline and their new baby brother, Steven, in the Groves Hospital obstetric ward. Pauline and Charles went on to have two more children after Steven: Clifford and Katherine, the youngest.

Since World War II had just ended on November 11th, 1944, there was still a prevailing sense of the need for preparedness in case of future conflicts. To promote readiness, organizations like Brownies, Guides, Cubs, and Scouts were established. Pauline and her sister Barbara decided to enroll their daughters Brenda and Connie in a nearby Brownie pack, which met weekly in a hall on Saint Andrew Street. However, they faced financial constraints and had to seek out affordable options for uniforms. They found a used Brownie uniform at the thrift shop sponsored by the hospital auxiliary and Pauline altered it to fit Brenda, hemming the dress as needed. The uniform included a straight brown shift with long sleeves, a darker brown tam, and a leather belt, along with breast pockets on the shift dress and a gold pixie pin on the tam.

At Brownies, the girls learned a variety of valuable skills such as cooking, cleaning, knitting, sewing, first aid, semaphore, and knot tying. Semaphore was a method used by ships to communicate with flags, while knot tying was essential for handling small watercraft. First aid training prepared the girls for potentially nursing wounded soldiers during wartime.

Each week, the girls walked to their Brownie meetings, where they were greeted by Brown Owl, Mrs. Cameron, and her assistant, Mrs. Barbara Morrison, who was Connie's mother. Barbara volunteered her time to instruct the same Brownie pack attended by her daughter and niece. The meetings typically began with the girls standing in a circle reciting the Brownie oath, followed by a chant imitating an owl's call. They then split into groups named after mythical creatures like pixies, fairies, or elves, where they were taught various skills by the leaders and other volunteer women.

Initially timid, Brenda's confidence grew over the years while attending Brownies. By the age of 11, she became the leader of the Pixies. However, her enthusiasm for Guides waned, leading her to quit much to Pauline's disappointment. Brenda and Connie earned numerous badges, which their mothers proudly sewed onto their uniforms. Brenda's knitting badge was earned for knitting a doll's hat and scarf, while her sewing badge came after correcting a hem on a doll's skirt under Brown Owl's guidance. Although Brenda felt her mother should not be earning badges for her, Barbara was excelling at earning even more badges for Connie, sparking a competitive spirit between Pauline and Barbara. However, Brenda's disinterest in Guides brought an end to this friendly competition.

Brenda progressed from kindergarten to Grade 1, where the children began learning the alphabet. Large printed letters adorned the walls above the blackboards, serving as constant reminders of their ABC's. In Grade 2, under Miss Bleuler's guidance, the children delved into reading short stories such as "Jack and Jill" and "See Spot Run," which were featured in their Grade 2 reading books. Brenda particularly admired the illustrations of Sally, a blonde girl with curls, and a black-and-white spaniel named Spot. However, she struggled with reading, prompting Miss Bleuler to suspect that Brenda couldn't see the blackboard. Miss Bleuler contacted Brenda's parents and recommended an eye exam with the town's optometrist, Mr. Dickey.

A week later, Brenda and her parents visited Mr. Dickey's office for the eye exam. The examination involved reading a chart with varying sizes of letters through a machine equipped with lenses of different strengths. It was confirmed that Brenda needed glasses. Brenda was apprehensive about wearing glasses, but her parents insisted. They ended up choosing a pair with blue horn-rimmed frames adorned with silver lightning-shaped lines.

The following day at school, during recess, a classmate taunted Brenda with the nickname "four eyes." Brenda's teacher overheard the exchange and reprimanded the boy. Although Brenda appreciated her teacher's support, being called "four eyes" intensified her dislike for her glasses. She started carrying them in her coat pocket instead of wearing them, and one day, she discovered them broken in her pocket. Fearful of her parents' reaction, Brenda concocted a story about dreaming of the glasses breaking, which her parents surprisingly believed. They bought her another pair with her father's hard-earned money.

As the school years passed, Brenda struggled in several subjects, especially spelling, due to her dyslexia. Reading and math also posed challenges, and she failed Grade 6. In the past, students who didn't pass were required to repeat the year. For Brenda, repeating Grade 6 was a blessing in disguise as it allowed her to improve her grades and gain a stronger academic foundation.

Brenda, true to her nature, ran to and from school every day to avoid interacting with other children. Although this might have seemed like a negative habit, it made her an exceptionally fast runner. This became evident during her Grade 6 year at a Field Day Event held in Victoria Park for the public school. Brenda participated in a relay race where three boys preceded her. The race involved passing a baton back and forth until each runner completed the course. Overhearing two boys ahead of her discussing the expectation that a girl would be the last to run the relay race on their team, Brenda felt determined to prove them wrong. When her turn came, she sprinted across the field, overtaking the other teams and leading her team to victory.

At the age of 13, Brenda still spent much of her time at Beatty Park, where she met a much younger neighbor named Murray Moffett, who was only 4 years old. Murray would follow her around like a lost puppy, often alone like Brenda. Murray lived across the street from the park in a beautiful gray stone house. His older brother Michael was supposed to be watching him, but Michael would leave Murray in the park to play with older boys his age. Brenda and Murray grew close, with Murray even expressing his intention to marry her when he grew up. Brenda indulged him, pushing him on a swing and listening to his stories.

Across the street from the Morrison family lived a spinster named Miss Stevenson, in a big brown brick home with cream trim, on a hill between Colquhoun Street and Saint Andrew. Brenda enjoyed helping her rake leaves in the fall. Miss Stevenson's property boasted many beautiful Sugar Maple trees, whose leaves turned a glorious red, gold, and orange shade after the first frosts of winter. Brenda and Miss Stevenson would rake the leaves into piles along the road and burn them. Brenda was rewarded for her work with Halloween candies, which she enjoyed while watching

Miss Stevenson tend the fire. Despite the modest reward, Brenda cherished the time spent with her neighbor.

However, Brenda's dreamy summer days at her favorite park and in her beloved neighborhood came to an end in her 13th year when the Morrison family moved to the South end of Fergus, near the high school Brenda would soon attend after their relocation to Albert St.

Brenda had grown into a lovely young lady with long, wavy brown hair, which she sometimes straightened by winding it around Campbell's soup cans after washing. She had dark brown, almost black eyes that were particularly beautiful when she smiled. Tall for her age, Brenda had a slim, athletic build and a beige complexion, with only the occasional zit. She enjoyed sports like basketball, gymnastics, baseball, and track and field, displaying a bit of a tomboyish nature. Her ancestry was a mix of Scottish, English, Irish, and Ojibway, sometimes humorously referred to as a "57 Heinz" due to the diversity of ingredients in Heinz soup.

Unlike most teenagers, Brenda tended to keep to herself, often considered a bit of a loner. However, she did enjoy spending time with her family, going to movies, and simply hanging out around the house. On one occasion, Charles took Brenda to see the movie "Journey to The Centre of the Earth" at the Grand Theater in town, where she was delighted to have her father's attention. For the outing, her mother had made her a lovely peach-striped shift dress with a matching cord belt, the latest fashion at the time.

During the summer, the Morrison family would occasionally pile into Charles' new green Chevrolet station wagon and head to the Mustang Drive-in on the east end of Guelph, a small city south of Fergus. Rodney and Steven would lay in the back of the station wagon on blankets in their pajamas, while Brenda sat in the back seat with Pauline and Charles in front, along with baby Clifford. Brenda's parents would instruct her to slouch down upon entering the drive-in so she could pass for a 12-year-old and avoid paying the adult ticket price. Brenda disliked this, finding it embarrassing, but complied nonetheless. However, she never got caught, as she always looked much younger than her age throughout her teenage years and even into her senior year.

High school initiation struck fear into the hearts of the grade nine students, and Brenda was no exception. Her group had to wear school beanies, described as "little black and yellow skullcaps," and march around the high school property. Brenda and her classmates had heard horror stories of initiation stunts being performed on grade nine students, but Brenda managed to avoid them by playing hooky for the rest of the day. She simply slipped out of line and headed home, as she only lived a block from the school. After initiation day, the students settled down to work.

Charles had a new job fixing appliances for GSW, and as he was often on the road, he picked up a fashionable black leather clutch purse with a chain handle for Brenda upon her graduation to high school. He thought Brenda would need it for her makeup, noticing her experimentation now that she was a teenager. Brenda was overwhelmed with gratitude and couldn't believe her father had thought to purchase such a wonderful and necessary gift for her. Inside the card, it said, "To my Princess with love." Brenda shyly thanked her father and gave him a little hug, as she was not very demonstrative when it came to hugs and kisses.

The Morrison family's house on Albert St was much bigger than their previous one on Colquhoun. With Charles' new position as an appliance repairman, they were able to pay off the mortgage and even buy a small cottage near Orillia, Ontario. It was a happy time for Charles, Pauline, and their five children. Summers were spent at the cottage on the Black River, swimming, hiking, and roasting hot dogs and marshmallows around a campfire were some of their favorite activities. Brenda still played with paper dolls during her first summer of grade nine at the cottage, but she put them away for good that summer of her 15th year.

In the fall of 1966, the entire student body of Fergus High School was engaged in a frantic race to raise enough funds so that all the students, all 1000 of them, could attend the Montreal Quebec exhibition, Expo, celebrating Canada's 100th birthday. They organized bake sales, car washes, and sold peanuts and chocolate bars, mostly to their families. The year 1967, when Fergus High School went to Expo, was a massive undertaking for teachers and students alike. Tickets were booked for all on a train from Guelph, and buses had to be arranged at both ends to transport the students to and from their accommodations and the exhibition grounds. For a week, they stayed in private homes, halls, and schools, laying sleeping bags on the floor and eating in cafeterias in some cases. They congregated at lunchtime in a parking lot at the exhibition grounds, where a box lunch with a ham and cheese sandwich, an apple, fruit turnover, and milk were delivered to each student from the trunk of a car. They ate the same lunch every day for a week, although some complained.

Brenda was billeted at a Catholic school run by nuns while her two girlfriends, with whom she toured the exhibition grounds, stayed elsewhere. They met up each day when their buses arrived and walked miles, touring the national and international exhibits. They carried autograph books to collect stamps from each exhibit as a memento of their visit. Brenda's favorite exhibit was Habitat for Humanity, a three-story apartment building constructed with box-shaped units staggered to provide privacy to their neighbors, although it looked somewhat confusing to live there.

The three girls, Barbara, Wendy, and Brenda, got very little sleep during that week. It passed in a blur of excitement and some stress, as none of the girls had been away from home without their parents for an extended length of time.

When it was time to go home, the buses picked the students up at their temporary residences and delivered them to the train station in Montreal. There, 1000 students climbed aboard and headed home to the Guelph station to be picked up by their families. Brenda slept all the way home, her head propped against the window, while exuberant student voices loudly exchanged stories of their visit to Montreal Expo 1967.